D1237376

THE CHRISTIAN CRUSADER ™

By JOHN CELESTRI

THE CHRISTIAN CRUSADER ADVENTURE ALBUM SERIES

BOOK I
THE QUEST BEGINS

BOOK II
WEB OF LIES...CHAINS OF SIN

BOOK III
PLAGUE OF EVIL

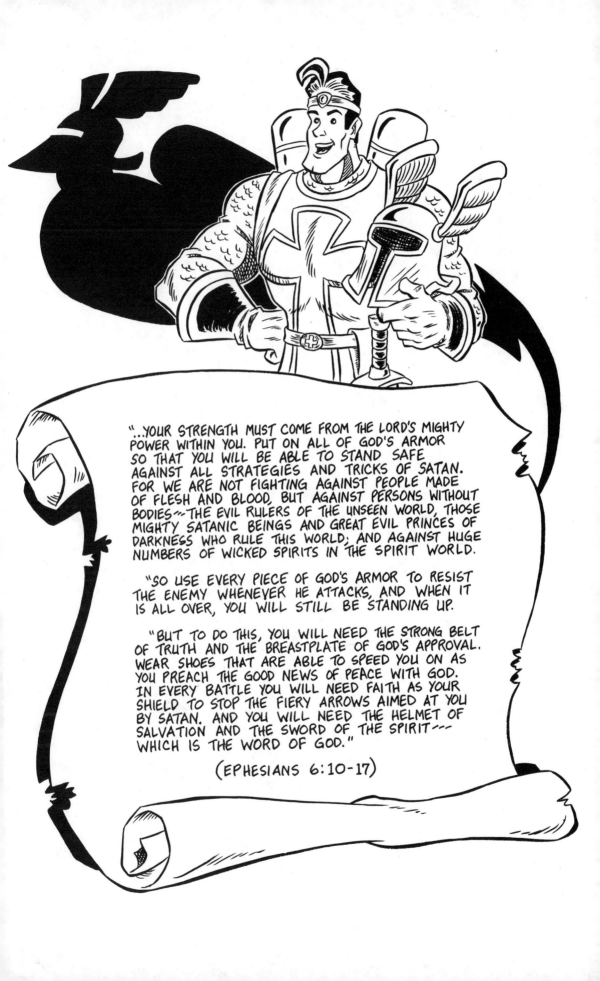

"...YOUR STRENGTH MUST COME FROM THE LORD'S MIGHTY POWER WITHIN YOU. PUT ON ALL OF GOD'S ARMOR SO THAT YOU WILL BE ABLE TO STAND SAFE AGAINST ALL STRATEGIES AND TRICKS OF SATAN. FOR WE ARE NOT FIGHTING AGAINST PEOPLE MADE OF FLESH AND BLOOD, BUT AGAINST PERSONS WITHOUT BODIES---THE EVIL RULERS OF THE UNSEEN WORLD, THOSE MIGHTY SATANIC BEINGS AND GREAT EVIL PRINCES OF DARKNESS WHO RULE THIS WORLD; AND AGAINST HUGE NUMBERS OF WICKED SPIRITS IN THE SPIRIT WORLD.

"SO USE EVERY PIECE OF GOD'S ARMOR TO RESIST THE ENEMY WHENEVER HE ATTACKS, AND WHEN IT IS ALL OVER, YOU WILL STILL BE STANDING UP.

"BUT TO DO THIS, YOU WILL NEED THE STRONG BELT OF TRUTH AND THE BREASTPLATE OF GOD'S APPROVAL. WEAR SHOES THAT ARE ABLE TO SPEED YOU ON AS YOU PREACH THE GOOD NEWS OF PEACE WITH GOD. IN EVERY BATTLE YOU WILL NEED FAITH AS YOUR SHIELD TO STOP THE FIERY ARROWS AIMED AT YOU BY SATAN. AND YOU WILL NEED THE HELMET OF SALVATION AND THE SWORD OF THE SPIRIT--- WHICH IS THE WORD OF GOD."

(EPHESIANS 6:10-17)

THE CHRISTIAN CRUSADER: PLAGUE OF EVIL
Copyright © and Trademark ™ 1994 by John Celestri.
All rights reserved.

Nothing may be reproduced in whole or in part without written
permission from the copyright owner.

Unless otherwise stated, all Scripture quotes are taken from The Living Bible © 1971.
Used by permission of Tyndale House Publishers, Inc., Wheaton, IL 60189.
All rights reserved.

Scripture quotations marked NIV are from the Holy Bible,
NEW INTERNATIONAL VERSION. Copyright © 1973, 1978, 1984
International Bible Society. Used by permission of
Zondervan Bible Publishers.

Verses marked (KJV) are taken from The King James Version of the Bible.

Front and back covers produced in conjunction
with ZENDER & ASSOCIATES, CINCINNATI, OHIO

Published by CC COMICS, PO Box 542, Loveland, Ohio 45140.

First Edition: September 1994

ISBN 0-9634183-3-5

Printed in the United States of America

ON THE OPPOSITE END OF THE UNIVERSE --- AT THE POINT FARTHEST FROM THE PLANET EARTH --- EXISTS A WORLD NAMED **THREA!**

THE **GOOD NEWS OF JESUS CHRIST** HAS BEEN SOWN THERE, BUT IT IS A WORLD OF ROCKY SOIL AND THERE ARE VERY FEW FERTILE SPOTS FOR **GOD'S SEED** (WORD) TO GROW! *

* MATTHEW 13:3

SATAN'S AGENT, **ZA-TIN THE UNHOLY ONE,** HAS CONQUERED ALL OF **THREA**....

1

EVERYTHING IS UNDER THE DOMINATION OF HIS IRON FIST---

EXCEPT FOR ONE PERSON...

THE CHRISTIAN CRUSADER!

SIR DAVID IS THE LAST KNIGHT OF CHRIST, AND AS THE CHRISTIAN CRUSADER HE DEDICATES HIS LIFE TO SPREADING THE WORD OF GOD...

...AND BATTLES THE FORCES OF EVIL AS A CHAMPION OF OUR LORD JESUS CHRIST!

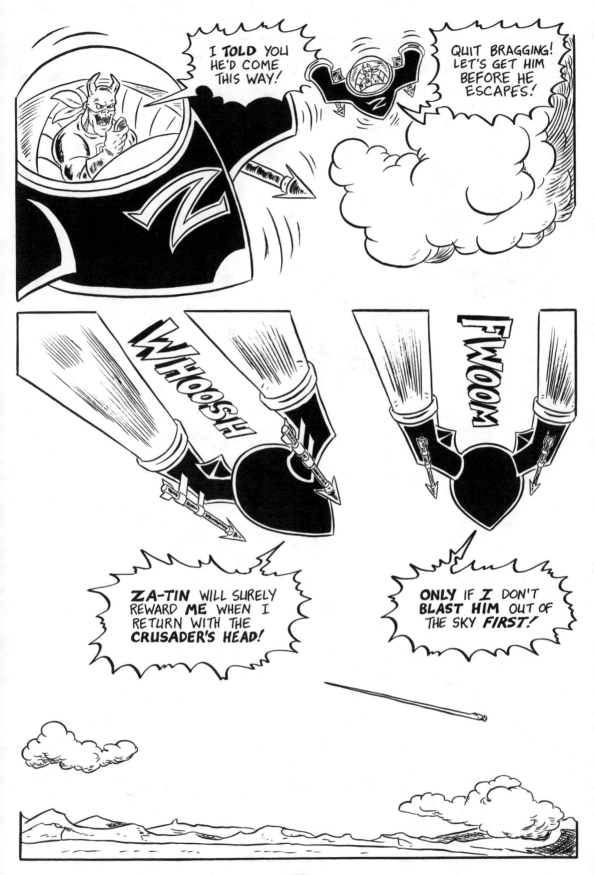

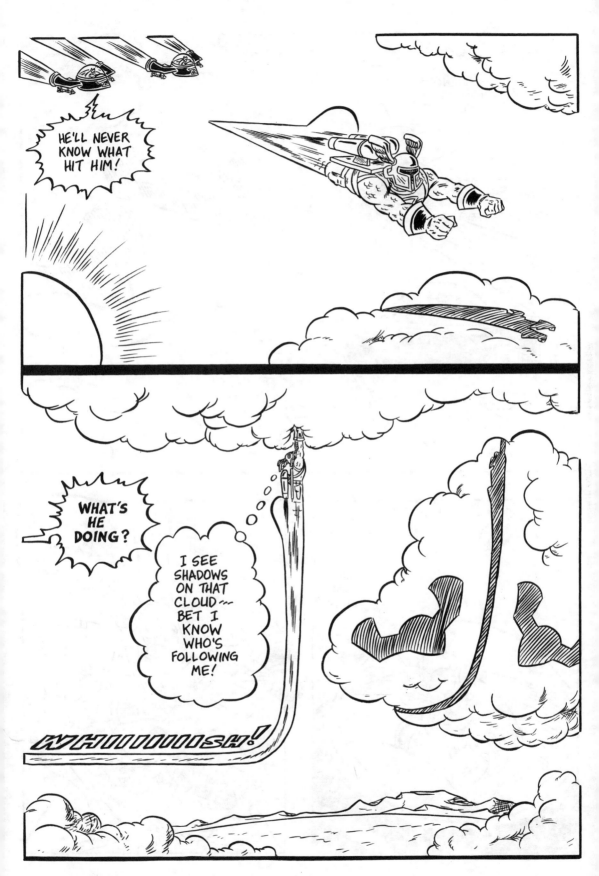

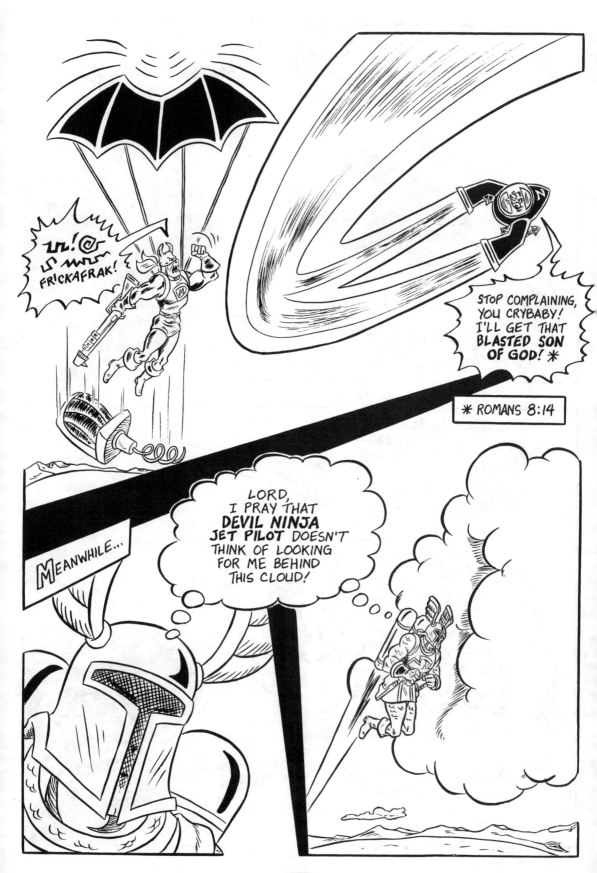

26

MANY POLITICIANS HAVE A PARTICULAR **WEAKNESS** FOR **MONEY**--- THE POTENTIAL FOR **SIN** IS **GREAT!**

I KNOW **THIS** MAYOR, AND WHEN **HE** GETS HIS HANDS ON THIS TREASURE CHEST, THE **COVET GAS** IS **SURE** TO WORK ON HIM....

...AND NOT ONLY ON **HIM** BUT ON **EVERYONE** HE ASSOCIATES WITH! **THE MORE PEOPLE** COME **UNDER THE INFLUENCE** OF THE **COVET GAS,** THE **MORE SIN** WILL SPREAD!

HAHAHA! HO!HO! HAAA!

38

CHAPTER 5

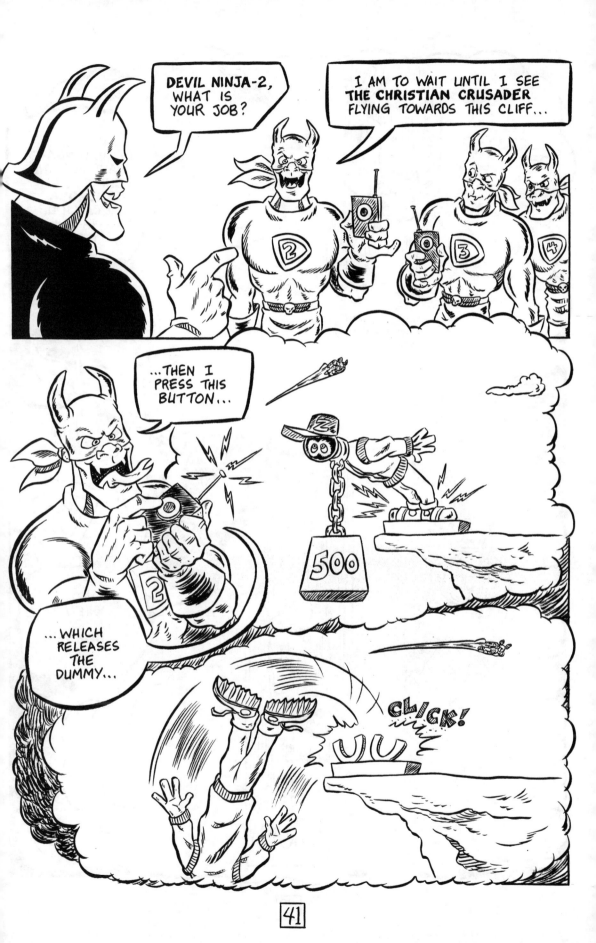

43

MEANWHILE, BACK AT ZA-TIN'S THRONE ROOM...
HA! HA! HA! IT'S WORKING!
CLAP! CLAP!
SIN! SIN! GLORIOUS SIN! WHAT STARTED AS COVETING AND ENVY HAS TURNED INTO GREED AND HATRED! I LOVE IT!

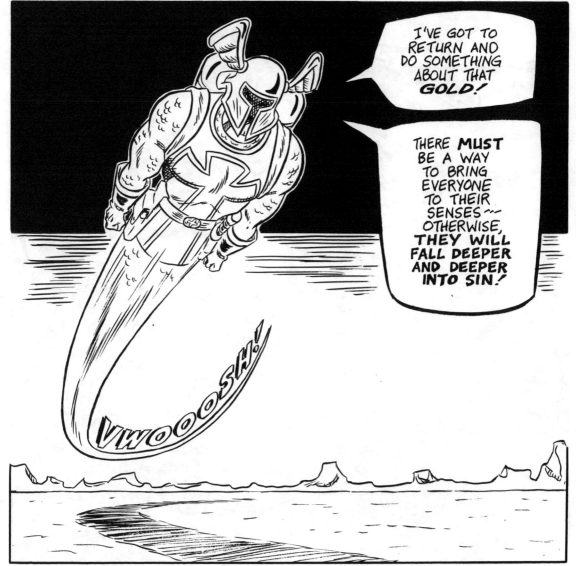